This story is dedicated to all the fairy lovers...

Nixie was Fairyland's master baker.

Her shop was always filled with fresh fairy-treats.

One day Nixie was asked to create a cake for the Fairy Queen's birthday party.

This was a great honour and she spent days preparing and working.

She even flew to the Great Mossy Mountains to collect rare ingredients.

When the baking was done, Nixie covered her cake with a cloth.

The Palace guards would arrive early in the morning to take it to the place where the party would be held.

No one would be able to take a peek until it was unveiled to the Fairy Queen.

The next morning Nixie got up early.

But when she walked into her kitchen, the cake was gone!

She froze, not sure what to do.

"My cake has been stolen!" she cried when the guards came.

The guards investigated the kitchen, but found nothing suspicious except for a faint smell of rotten frogs hanging in the air.

Suddenly Nixie's friend Bennie rushed in, out of breath.

"I was taking my pixie-dog for a walk, and I saw a troll pulling an old wagon. It had something in it, covered by a cloth. A cloth like the one you made for the Queen's cake!"

Everyone ran outside, where they found some **HUGE** footprints.

They followed the trail and soon caught up with the thief.

The guards ran after the troll and stopped him.

Looking scared, he confessed that he'd sneaked into Nixie's shop just before dawn to steal a cake for the Troll Queen's birthday.

"We've been baking to surprise the Troll Queen with a cake, but we're no good at it!" sobbed the troll. Green bubbles were coming out of his nostrils.

"Don't cry, Mister Troll," Nixie said in a gentle voice. "When is your queen's birthday?"

"In a week's time. We need the cake to be mouldy by then."

"Then I'll tell you what, Mr Troll..."

"Call me Stinkers," he interrupted.

"If you give this cake back, Stinkers, you can come to my kitchen after our queen's party and we can bake another one for your troll queen."

"Yippee!" cried Stinkers, and gave the cake back right away.

All the fairies enjoyed the celebrations.

The Queen **especially** loved her birthday cake.

She gave Nixie a rare jewel to thank her for her baking,

and for...

... helping the trolls bake a cake for **their** queen too!

Printed in Great Britain
by Amazon